Dance
ike a
Leaf

For my
Grandma Jeanne
— AJ Irving

For my kids,
Paula and
Santiago
— Claudia Navarro

Barefoot Books
2067 Massachusetts Ave
Cambridge, MA 02140

Barefoot Books
29/30 Fitzroy Square
London, W1T 6LQ

Text copyright © 2020 by
AJ Irving. Illustrations copyright
© 2020 by Claudia Navarro
The moral rights of AJ Irving
and Claudia Navarro
have been asserted

First published in United
States of America by Barefoot
Books, Inc and in Great Britain
by Barefoot Books, Ltd in 2020
All rights reserved

Graphic design by
Sarah Soldano, Barefoot Books
Edited and art directed by
Kate DePalma, Barefoot Books
Reproduction by Bright Arts,
Hong Kong

Printed in China on
100% acid-free paper
This book was typeset in
Foglihten and Meridien
The illustrations were prepared in
acrylics with digital retouching

Hardback ISBN
978-1-64686-057-9
Paperback ISBN
978-1-64686-058-6
E-book ISBN
978-1-64686-015-9

British Cataloguing-in-
Publication Data: a catalogue
record for this book is available
from the British Library

Library of Congress Cataloging-
in-Publication Data is available
under LCCN 2020005227

1 3 5 7 9 8 6 4 2

Dance like a Leaf

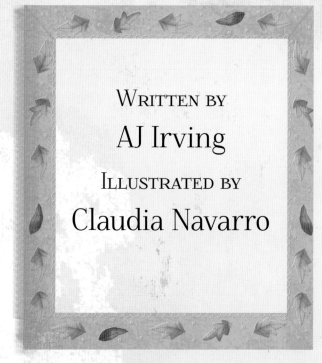

WRITTEN BY

AJ Irving

ILLUSTRATED BY

Claudia Navarro

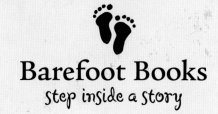

Barefoot Books
step inside a story

September.
Green goes to sleep.
Yellow sings a sweet melody.

Grandma loves autumn.

We sip our tea.

"Tea makes your tummy toasty," Grandma says.

We bundle up.
"The more scarves, the better," Grandma says.

We wave to the trees.
"Hello trees!" Grandma says.

We sing with the breeze.
"Soft and sweet," Grandma says.

And we twirl under falling leaves.
"Dance like a leaf!" Grandma says.

October.

Orange and red join the chorus.

Grandma forgets the teacups,
so I put two on our special table.
"Does your tummy feel toasty?" I ask.
"Oh, yes!" Grandma says.

Grandma forgets her scarves.
"I think you need three," I say.
"I think you're right," Grandma says.

Grandma's eyes aren't sparkly, so I cheer her up.
"Look at all the orange leaves!" I say.
"How lovely," Grandma says.
But Grandma doesn't wave to the trees.

"Hello trees!" I say.
Grandma doesn't sing with the breeze.
"Sing with me, Grandma!"
She watches the leaves but doesn't dance.
"Like this, Grandma!"

November.
Burgundy leaves hum softly, curling at the ends.
Crisp and fragile, they hang by a thread.

Grandma stays in bed.

We don't sip tea.

We don't bundle up in scarves.

We don't wave or sing or dance.

Instead, I paint her trees from memory.

"What a beautiful painting," Grandma whispers.
Grandma smiles as she drifts off to sleep.
I think she's dreaming of dancing with me.

December.
Nearly naked trees shed the last of their leaves.

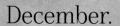

Grandma's bed is empty.

Our teacups sit in a tidy stack.
Our scarves hang like a rainbow, quiet but vibrant.

Winter turns to spring,
spring turns to summer,
and summer turns to autumn.

Grandma loved autumn.

I sip my tea.

I bundle up.
I wave to the trees.
I sing with the breeze.
I dance like a leaf...

…just like Grandma taught me.